917.7 Lou
Lourie, Peter.
Mississippi River

W9-CDI-200

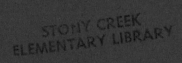
STONY CREEK
ELEMENTARY LIBRARY

MISSISSIPPI RIVER

"The face of the water, in time, became a wonderful book—a book that was a dead language to the uneducated passenger, but which told its mind to me without reserve, delivering its most cherished secrets as if it uttered them with a voice. And it was not a book to be read once and thrown aside, for it had a new story to tell every day."

—from *Life on the Mississippi* by Mark Twain (1883)

MISSISSIPPI RIVER

A Journey Down the Father of Waters

PETER LOURIE

BOYDS MILLS PRESS

MISSISSIPPI RIVER

The Mississippi River runs approximately 2,340 miles from Lake Itasca in Minnesota to the Gulf of Mexico. The Big River drains a massive area that measures about 1.25 million square miles. With its chief tributaries, the Missouri and Ohio Rivers, the Mississippi forms the third-largest river basin in the world, after the Nile and the Amazon.

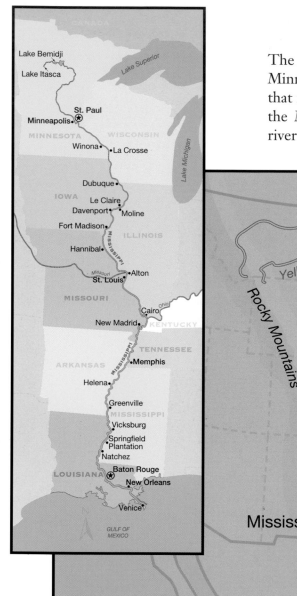

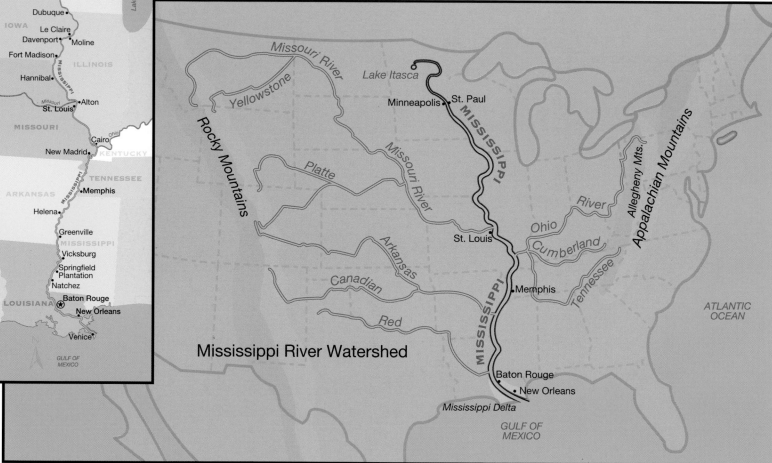

Mississippi River Watershed

Contents

PROLOGUE

FOR YEARS I WANTED TO canoe the Mississippi, but was afraid to paddle the Big River. The Mississippi seemed larger than life. Yet I knew one day I would need to feel the river under my canoe. That's the best way for me to understand rivers. So after traveling the Amazon, the Hudson, the Yukon, and other rivers, I decided it was time to meet the Father of Waters.

One September, I set out on my Mississippi journey. I started near Canada at Lake Itasca, the river's modest source. I traveled by canoe, bike, and car all the way down to the Gulf of Mexico, where the massive waters of the river are swallowed by an even greater sea. My goal was to follow the river, dive into it, float on it, talk to the people who worked on it. In this way, I hoped to gain some understanding of America's greatest waterway.

At first, I felt at home in the pines and the loon-calling mists at the river's Minnesota headwaters. But as I traveled south of Minneapolis, I began to feel overwhelmed by the size of the locks; the giant, barge-pushing tows; the broad width of the flood plain; and the deceptive calm of the evenings. When I paddled onto the big flat water at dusk, something mysterious seemed to lie just below the surface—as if Scotland's Loch Ness monster had a Mississippi cousin lurking beneath my boat.

"Big River," or *Misizubi*, which is Algonquian for "a river spread over a large area," splices the United States together, running down the center of the country like a giant zipper. With a length of approximately 2,340 miles from Lake Itasca, Minnesota, to the Gulf of Mexico, the Mississippi is the second-longest river in the United States, exceeded only by the Missouri. This heartland river touches ten states and drains thirty-one. Trickling from its source at Lake Itasca, it grows and grows until it pours more than three hundred billion gallons of water into the Gulf each day. Its tributaries and feeder streams stretch all the way from New York to Montana—from the Alleghenies to the Rockies.

Was I prepared to tackle the mighty Mississippi?

PART ONE

Headwaters of the Mississippi

LAKE ITASCA

I LEFT THE EAST COAST WITH MY PADDLING PARTNER, Ernie LaPrairie, and drove to northern Minnesota. We began our Mississippi journey at Lake Itasca, the river's source. Near the Canadian border, surrounded by red and white pines, Itasca is a watery gem in a land of timber wolves, moose, black bear, eagles, and snowy owls.

LaPrairie dropped our thirty-eight-pound, seventeen-foot canoe into the lake, and we stroked in unison as the call of a loon pierced the cold, northern silence. Paddling through the early morning mist felt magical. Overhead, Canada geese arrowed southward.

The Ojibwe people migrated into the Itasca area hundreds of years ago to harvest wild rice and to hunt and fish. They called this lake *Omushkos*, meaning elk. French fur trappers called it *Lac la Biche*, "elk lake." The name changed, however, when the Ojibwe guide Ozawindib led Henry Rowe Schoolcraft to Omushkos in July 1832. Schoolcraft, who was searching for the source of the Mississippi, determined that

Coming upon a beaver lodge.

This painting shows how the Ojibwe people gathered rice long ago.

Lac la Biche was where the Big River began. In honor of his discovery, he renamed it Itasca, which is a combination of two Latin words, *veritas* and *caput*, "truth" and "head." Hence verITAS CAput, or Itasca, the true head of the Mississippi.

Low Water and Wild Rice

Because the summer had been dry, very little water flowed over the line of rocks that marked the Mississippi outlet. We dragged our canoe over the shallows and started to paddle through the tiniest of channels. The first mile of the river was no wider than the canoe itself.

The river meandered in almost 360-degree loops. LaPrairie, in the bow, had to pull hard with his paddle to navigate the canoe around the hairpin turns. Minnows darted in front of us like streaks of black paint. Blue herons sprang raucously into the air, and painted turtles dove off logs as we passed.

Just when we thought we'd found a clear channel, we came crashing to a halt on top of a beaver dam. We'd taken the wrong fork, and the river had run out of water. I now had to scout the river in search of another route, struggling through eight-foot-high sedge that cut the skin around my sandals.

The low water, however, meant a good wild rice harvest for the Ojibwe, who have the right to harvest rice here, as well as on their nearby reservations. August is known as the "rice moon," the time of the ripening of wild rice.

The Ojibwe still gather rice in the traditional way. One

The traditional rice-gathering method is used today.

Coffee Pot Landing: taking a break from paddling.

person gently poles a canoe through a stand of wild rice, and another person in the bow holds a short stick in each hand. One stick is used for bending the stalks over the boat, while the other stick is used to draw the rice off the stalks and into a pile on the canoe floor.

By late afternoon, we were exhausted from maneuvering the canoe through the low water. The river widened to about sixteen feet across but remained only knee deep. We dragged the canoe over rocky sections. When the river got deeper, I watched the long strands of water celery wave just below the surface like women's hair. The lovely green eelgrass leaned forward in the clear stream, directing us southward, as the river picked up speed and volume.

Just before dark, we were relieved to find a good place to camp called Coffee Pot Landing. Coffee Pot Landing is rumored to have gotten its name from an old coffee pot that hung on a tree near the river's shore. Stories have it that the pot was left there to mark the spot. Others say it was here for people like Ernie and me to use while taking a break at the landing. We didn't find the pot, but we did make coffee with our own big pot.

Logging

The next morning we came out of the dense vegetation of the first section of the river and into a bright, wide expanse of open water, Lake Bemidji. Here the river, now flowing east-

Lake Bemidji: paddling through stands of wild rice.

A monument to Paul Bunyan and Babe, his blue ox, stands on the shore of Lake Bemidji.

ward, opened into a series of lakes before turning south. Legend says that Lake Bemidji was formed when the mythic lumberjack Paul Bunyan put his giant foot into the mud.

This was old logging country. During the log drives, when the river and lakes filled with melting snow in the spring, the logs were floated downstream to the sawmills. The lakes acted as holding pens for the timber. It must have been an impressive sight to see all those logs from shore to shore, like a pile of titan pickup sticks.

River Rats, as the men who lived and worked on the river called themselves, guided the logs along their way with pike poles and peaveys, which are something like harpoons and giant fishhooks. These agile men, wearing spiked boots, jumped from log to log. If they fell into the icy river and didn't get out quickly enough, they were in danger of freezing to death.

At Wolf Lake, big waves made canoeing tough, but we managed to stay dry, until we ended the long day at an Ojibwe cemetery on Lake Andrusia. The shallow wooden graves looked like little houses. They were lined up in rows on the forest floor. Each had a small opening at the end, a window for mourners to insert offerings of wild rice. We did not linger in this sacred place.

Only a few days into our trip, and the leaves seemed to be turning yellow and red by the hour. So LaPrairie and I headed south, fleeing the coming of autumn in the north country.

Logjam on the Mississippi near Little Falls, Minnesota, around 1905.

PART TWO

The Upper Mississippi: River of Commerce

LOCKS AND DAMS

WE DROVE DOWN TO THE TWIN CITIES of Minneapolis and St. Paul to find that some four hundred miles after the river leaves Itasca, the Mississippi has become a major river. As we approached Minneapolis–St. Paul, we passed by dams and energy plants.

At Minneapolis I tried my portable bike for the first time. This little bicycle was an efficient way to explore river towns and cities. Weighing only twenty pounds and folding into a case the size of a duffel bag, it fit nicely inside the canoe.

I rode my bike to the first lock on the river—an enormous four-hundred-foot-long chamber at St. Anthony Falls. Because of growing river commerce and heavy damages from floods, in 1879 the U. S. Congress established the Mississippi River Commission, whose goals were to deepen the shipping channel, protect riverbanks, improve navigation, and prevent river flooding. As part of this program, the U.S. Army Corps of Engineers built twenty-nine locks and dams on the upper river from Minneapolis down to St. Louis, Missouri, a distance of

My portable bike was a handy way to explore what lay beyond the river.

Lock at St. Anthony Falls: down in the chamber after the release of millions of gallons of water.

669 miles with a drop in elevation of 420 feet. This series of locks, or steps, requires boats to either climb as they travel upstream or descend as they move downstream.

I folded up my bike, got in the canoe, and paddled into the giant lock. I'd paddled the locks of the Erie and Champlain canals, but none was as big as this one. The upstream V gates opened like a giant's mouth to let me in. When they closed, a ghostly moaning rose from the valves opening somewhere below me, and the water rushed downstream out of the lock. Eleven million gallons were displaced for my tiny canoe. The water bubbled and gurgled. As the Big River shoved against the upstream gates, the metal made a creaky sound, as if the gates could break at any moment to let the whole Mississippi come crashing in on me.

In no more than eight minutes, I dropped nearly fifty feet. The doors swung silently open. Free of that slimy dungeon, I paddled happily into the big, bright river.

Mystery

Below St. Paul, sand-colored limestone bluffs mark the sides of the wide flood plain, where the river used to wander at will from channel to channel. For thousands of years the Mississippi shifted course and found the shortest way to the sea, often creating its giant meandering loops called oxbows. When the river decided to cut through the neck of the loops, it formed lakes known as oxbow lakes.

An egret takes flight.

Saying good-bye to Ernie.

The river had always shortened and lengthened itself at will, adding or subtracting hundreds of miles. But no longer can it do so. To control flooding and facilitate shipping, engineers now determine the Big River's course. Only in times of flood does the river overflow and once again go its own way.

In the town of Winona, Minnesota, LaPrairie and I visited the factory where our sleek canoe was made. Then we had a good long paddle into the evening. This would be our last time together because LaPrairie had to return to his family, and I planned to go on alone for the remainder of the trip.

As the sun set behind the bluffs, we floated out on the gentle current. We spent hours exploring sandbars and islands in the braided river. Like Huck Finn and Tom Sawyer, we sneaked up on some nesting cormorants, which filled the trees like Christmas decorations. The Mississippi Valley from Canada to the Gulf of Mexico is a major flyway for migratory birds. We watched hundreds of white pelicans, gulls, ducks, geese, and egrets fly helter-skelter through the deepening twilight.

Just before we finished paddling in the dark, something surfaced next to the canoe. We heard a loud splash. LaPrairie laughed when I called it a Mississippi mud monster. I always had the feeling of something large looming just beneath the canoe. I wondered what mysteries lay in the mud. Certainly there were steamboat wrecks down there, maybe hundreds.

The next morning, I said good-bye to my friend and headed south over the Iowa border.

Steamboats

In the 1800s you could see the plumes of steam rise from the water long before you heard the paddle wheelers chugging upriver. When steamboats arrived, sleepy river towns came awake with activity and excitement. Paddle wheelers carried merchants, immigrants, farmers, soldiers, slaves, gamblers, and swindlers. They also transported cotton, livestock, hay, corn, dry goods, wines, and luxuries from the docks of New Orleans. Steamboats were sometimes called "floating palaces" or "wedding cakes" because of their ornate woodwork. Mark Twain, who was himself a steamboat pilot, caught the excitement of steamboating in many of his books:

> *"Steamboats passed up and down every hour or so. Those belonging to the little Cairo line and the little Memphis line always stopped; the big Orleans liners stopped for hails only, or to land passengers or freight; and this was the case also with the great flotilla of 'transients.' These latter came out of a dozen rivers—the Illinois, the Missouri, the Upper Mississippi, the Ohio, the Monongahela, the Tennessee, the Red River, the White River, and so on; and were bound every whither and stocked with every imaginable comfort or necessity which the Mississippi's communities could want, from the frosty Falls of St. Anthony down through nine climates to torrid New Orleans."*
>
> —*from* Pudd'nhead Wilson *by Mark Twain (1894)*

A paddle wheeler on the old Mississippi.

*Today some boats, like the one below, run into trouble,
just as boats did years ago.*

The lives of steamboats were short. The greatest danger was fire from their huge boilers. But the river itself also threatened them with sandbars, snags, ice jams, rapids, low water, storms, and floods. One stretch of the river, from St. Louis to Cairo, Illinois, was so dangerous that rivermen called it the "graveyard." In 1867 at least 133 sunken hulks littered this short section of the Mississippi.

Steamboats carried goods and passengers, but they also carried such highly contagious diseases as cholera. Sometimes the boats pulled over to shore to bury victims of the disease. Other times, the dead were simply cast into the water.

In the nineteenth century, steamboats battled strong rapids and currents. Today those rapids have disappeared. When the Corps of Engineers built its locks and dams to aid navigation, the rising water covered a fifteen-mile rapid above Davenport, Iowa.

Driving logs in days of old.

Steamer with Log Raft on Mississippi River.

Jim Bailie

Lonestar: *the only wooden paddle wheeler to survive intact.*

Lonestar

Neighboring Le Claire is where the pilots lived who guided the paddle wheelers downriver through this treacherous section.

At the Buffalo Bill Museum in Le Claire, I met Jim Bailie, whose ancestors had been river pilots. I could tell Jim loved steamers. He explained how two steamers worked to drive logs down through the rapids in the late 1800s. One steamer would push the raft of logs from behind, while another, positioning itself sideways to the river in front of the logs, helped steer the load right or left by thrusting its engines forward or backward. All communication between the steamers was done by horns and whistles. There were no marine radios in those days.

Jim took me to see the *Lonestar*, a paddle wheeler that once plied the Mississippi. Today the old ship is preserved on shore. It is more than a hundred years old—an amazing feat considering the ship's hull is made of wood instead of steel.

In the pilothouse.

A levee washed away by the river.

In fact, the *Lonestar* is the only wood-hulled, paddle wheel boat in the United States that has remained intact.

From the deck, I looked out on the river, where the powerful boat once chugged and churned. Then Jim took me down to the engine room to see the boiler and gages and gears. But the best part was climbing up top to sit in the pilot's chair. I took the wheel, and for a few minutes imagined myself piloting a paddle wheeler on the Big River.

Le Claire is also the birthplace of William F. "Buffalo Bill" Cody. Born in a log cabin in Le Claire in 1846, Buffalo Bill moved to Kansas to become a pony express rider at age eleven. Later he became a guide for the railroad and the army. The great Sioux chief Sitting Bull was among the two hundred Native Americans he brought to Paris and London with his Wild West Show.

Floods

In Fort Madison, Iowa, I found evidence of the big flood of 1993. High-water marks could be found far back from where the river runs today. Floods are not new to the Mississippi. The river has flooded many times over the years. When it rises, the river has nowhere to go but over the smaller agricultural levees and into the areas where people have settled. The flood of 1927 was one of the worst. Cities and towns and farms were destroyed. More than two hundred people died.

A midwestern flood is not sudden like a hurricane. It builds for weeks and even months in advance. In 1993, as a result of unusual amounts of spring and summer rain, and also because of the runoff from large snow build-up in the north and west, the river rose through the summer, until the water overcame some of the levees. Fields and towns were awash in water.

By August of 1993, the water level finally began to drop. When it was all over, fifty thousand homes had been destroyed, and fifty people had died. The total cost of the '93 flood was in the billions of dollars.

A flooded street in Hughes, Arkansas, 1927.

Mark Twain

Mark Twain

The Mississippi River has inspired many authors, but none more famous than Mark Twain.

Mark Twain's real name was Samuel Clemens, but when he became a writer he took the pseudonym of Mark Twain, which was the river call for a water depth of two fathoms, or twelve feet. As a boy in Hannibal, Missouri, Twain was enraptured every time a steamboat came to town. He dreamed of becoming a steamboat pilot. The steamboat pilot was the king of the river, leading an exciting but dangerous life.

From Hannibal, I paddled far out into the Big River to an island closer to the Illinois shore. Some say this is the island that inspired Jackson's Island in Mark Twain's great novel *The Adventures of Huckleberry Finn*. It's the place where Huck and Jim meet before they head downriver on their raft. Twain spent his boyhood years rambling along the river and crossing over by canoe to this very island. I canoed around, then set up camp on a sandbar.

It was a thrill to lie on the sand at the tip of the island, reading passages from *Huckleberry Finn*. I looked out of my tent at the stars above and wondered if young Mark Twain had camped on this very spot.

Although Twain lived here about 150 years ago, his river world seemed not to have changed all that much. Mark Twain's Mississippi was still here.

Huck: from the original edition.

"... we run nights, and laid up and hid day-times; soon as night was most gone, we stopped navigating and tied up ....Then we set out the lines. Next we slid into the river and had a swim, so as to freshen up and cool off; then we set down on the sandy bottom where the water was about knee-deep, and watched the daylight come. Not a sound anywheres—perfectly still—just like the whole world was asleep, only sometimes the bullfrogs a-clattering, maybe."

—*from* The Adventures of Huckleberry Finn
by Mark Twain (1884)

I wondered if Mark Twain had camped on this very spot.

25

The arch at St. Louis.

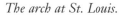

The arch at St. Louis.

The meeting of two great rivers—the Missouri (entering from the left) and the Mississippi.

The Missouri River

Just north of St. Louis, I passed the mouth of the Missouri River. At 2,540 miles, from its highest pond source to its confluence with the Mississippi, the Missouri is the longest river in the United States. Entering from the west, the Missouri turns the Mississippi a yellow, muddy brown. It is from these muddy deposits of the Missouri River that the Mississippi sometimes derives its name Big Muddy.

A few miles past the confluence of America's two greatest rivers, I came into the metropolis of St. Louis, Missouri. Paddling under the 630-foot silver arch on the St. Louis waterfront made me feel very small.

Marquette and Joliet descending the Mississippi. They were the first to record accurate information about the river.

I rode my bike around the bustling streets of the city. It was hard to imagine this was once wilderness. In 1673, the French explorers Father Jacques Marquette and Louis Joliet passed by the site of the future city while paddling down the Mississippi, looking for a westward passage to China. When the two Frenchmen passed the Missouri River a few miles upstream, they described how that other great river had nearly capsized their canoe. They called the Missouri a "savage river . . . a torrent of yellow mud . . . furiously athwart the calm blue current of the Mississippi, boiling and surging and sweeping in its course logs, branches, and uprooted trees."

Marquette and Joliet were the first Europeans to travel down the Mississippi as far as Arkansas. When they realized this was not the route they sought, they headed back to Quebec. A few years later, the explorer La Salle traveled the river down to the Gulf of Mexico and claimed the Mississippi watershed for France, calling the region "Louisiana."

In 1803, Napoleon sold the Louisiana Territory to President Thomas Jefferson, and the newly formed United States more than doubled its size overnight. The following year, Lewis and Clark and the Corps of Discovery departed from St. Louis, leaving the known world behind. They traveled up the Missouri River, over the Continental Divide in present-day Idaho, and down the Salmon, Snake, and Columbia Rivers to the Pacific Ocean. During their remarkable two-year expedition, they recorded in their journals previously undocumented information about the native people, wildlife, and plants of the West.

PART THREE

The Lower Mississippi: Old Man River

TOWBOATS AND THE RIVER CHANNEL

AFTER ST. LOUIS, the river runs free to the Gulf. No more dams, no more locks. The current grows even stronger, the water more massive, and the tows more numerous. I had been warned that if I didn't respect the lower Mississippi, it would swallow me up for sure.

Tows are tugboats that push barges up and down the river. In the old days they used to pull them and today are still called tows. The average towboat, a snub-nosed and rather boxy-looking vessel, might be 170 feet long and 45 feet wide, driven by two 5,000-horsepower diesel engines.

On the lower river, these tows are frightening. A thirty-barge tow is common today. Those thirty barges can carry 45,000 tons of goods, which is equal to 450 boxcars or 1,800 truckloads of material. Some tows can push as many as seventy barges at one time! Coal, gasoline, and fuel from the oil fields of Texas and Louisiana are shipped upriver. Downriver the tows carry such grains as corn, wheat, oats, barley, and rye loaded onto barges from elevators along shore.

The U.S. Army Corps of Engineers at work on the Mississippi.

The grain is transferred to ocean-going vessels in the port of New Orleans, then shipped overseas.

The Army Corps works around the clock to maintain a nine-foot-deep shipping channel. To provide flood protection, a levee system that is longer than the Great Wall of China has been constructed. These artificial riverbanks keep the river following the same route year after year. Today, there are sixteen hundred miles of levees along the river.

In addition to levees, the Corps has built dikes, rock structures that stick out into the river from shore. They keep the water flowing in such a way that sediment does not fill the channel. But even with all these devices, the Mississippi still carries millions of tons of sediment, and deposits this sediment in places that impede the prescribed channel. So the engineers regularly dredge the river to keep the shipping channel open. The New Orleans office of the Army Corps operates seven dredges around the clock to keep the channel from silting over.

The Ohio River

At Fort Defiance in Cairo, Illinois, I stood on a spit of land where the Mississippi is joined by the Ohio River. The Ohio is the Mississippi's biggest eastern tributary, and I was amazed that one-third of the nation's water was now flowing past me. With the Ohio's water, the newly invigorated Mississippi becomes a mass of bubbling liquid like a small, angry sea. I was now afraid to paddle in the center of this river. From here onward I vowed to hug the shore, where I would feel safer, out of the torrent and away from the tows.

Paddling south of Cairo, I kept my eyes peeled for the water moccasins that live in backwater swamps. The canoe handled sluggishly in the great churn of mud and silt. Whenever I went past a tow, I turned the canoe directly into the tow's wake and struggled not to tip over.

Fort Defiance, Cairo, Illinois: from my left, the Ohio River joining the Mississippi.

Earthquake and a Union Canal

I looked in vain for evidence of the terrible earthquake that had hit New Madrid, Missouri, in 1811. The shock waves were felt as far away as Montana and Washington, D.C.

STONY CREEK
ELEMENTARY LIBRARY

Union soldiers dug this canal during the Civil War.

Records show that when the quake hit, the river foamed up like water in a boiling cauldron. Water and steam and sulfur and sand spewed out of the earth. The river even ran backward!

In a local museum, I learned that during the Civil War the Union forces had built a canal that cut off the river bend. This enabled Union troops to attack an island that was heavily fortified by the South. It was a key victory in the Union's desire to control the Mississippi River.

The Union wanted to take control of the Mississippi from Cairo down to the Gulf, nearly one thousand miles of meandering river. New Madrid was especially important. Confederates tried to hold onto both the town and island upriver called Island Number 10 (the tenth island below the confluence of the Ohio and the Mississippi), but Union forces quickly took the town and then built a six-mile-long canal in nineteen days through a swamp in order to come around Island Number 10. The canal essentially cut off the wide bend in the river and allowed Federal forces to send troops north to attack the island from both sides. The Rebels finally gave up in 1862, and when Island Number 10 fell, the river was open for Union forces all the way to Vicksburg.

I paddled a piece of the canal, where the water ran swiftly. There was no one around, and it seemed incredible that the canal was still here. I felt as if I were paddling into history.

Houseboat at New Madrid, Missouri.

PART FOUR

The Mississippi Delta

WHITE GOLD

BELOW MEMPHIS, TENNESSEE, I entered the Mississippi Delta region, where the river has been depositing rich soil for thousands of years. It was here that the first European set eyes on the Mississippi in 1541. The Spanish conquistador Hernando de Soto, while searching for gold, crossed the river just below Memphis. Later he sickened and died, and his body was dropped into the Big River.

I followed the left bank of the river through the state of Mississippi, then, just above Vicksburg, crossed into Louisiana where the cotton was in full bloom. I could smell the light, fresh fragrance of ripe cotton everywhere. It was harvest time. I saw cotton flying off the backs of trucks like snow, cotton lying on the roads, cotton floating in the wind like pollen. If I had come down the river before the Civil War, the sight would have been different. I would have seen slaves in the fields picking cotton. Cotton, or "white gold," and the South's dependence on slave labor to harvest it, helped lead to the

This picture from Harper's Weekly, *March 7, 1863, shows the United States gunboat* Indianola *running the blockade at Vicksburg.*

terrible Civil War. Today, the grand plantations are greatly reduced in size, and machines have replaced the work of humans.

Battle of Vicksburg

In Vicksburg, Mississippi, I walked along the Confederate and Union fortifications, miles of trenches where so much blood was shed—in total, nearly twenty thousand dead, missing, or wounded. The forest had grown up over the battlefield, and it was hard to imagine the tragic scene.

Vicksburg, 437 miles from the Gulf, sits high on a bluff over a wide bend in the river. It was the last great river stronghold of the Confederates. The South held the town against Union forces for forty-seven days. Union gunboats pummeled the city from the river while the troops charged from their trenches over and over again, and died in great numbers. Still, the people of Vicksburg hung on. Finally, on July 4, 1863, the city surrendered. It was a bitter defeat for the Rebels. Now the Mississippi was controlled by the North.

A treasure from the Civil War may still lie beneath the river, deep in the Mississippi mud. Bound for Vicksburg and Grant's victorious Union Army, the steamer *Ruth* left the St. Louis riverfront on August 3, 1863, with 2.6 million dollars in cash aboard. A few days later, just south of Cairo, the *Ruth* caught fire, perhaps with the help of Confederate agents. The boat sank in only eighteen feet of water. Treasure hunters are

Hernando de Soto: the first European to set eyes on the Mississippi.

The Union cemetery at Vicksburg.

convinced that some strongboxes escaped the flames and are still hidden in the Mississippi mud.

In the afternoon I walked through the Union graveyard with its countless white gravestones, some with names, others just numbers. An eerie peace hung over the lonely mass of graves.

This photograph of slaves was taken in Louisiana sometime in 1863, the same year of Abraham Lincoln's Emancipation Proclamation. His decree abolished slavery in the Confederate states, but it did not take effect until 1865 with the end of the Civil War.

Tows and barges move up and down the Mississippi.

Hard at work on a barge.

Towboat

One day I was invited aboard a working towboat called the *Gilda Sherden*, a 1947 vessel that had seen many ports. Up in the pilothouse, James Butler, the pilot, showed me how to operate the spotlights and the rudder levers as he maneuvered three jumbo-size tank barges that would be filled with asphalt. Tonight he would begin to take his tow a thousand miles up the Mississippi, Ohio, and Tennessee Rivers to Chattanooga, Tennessee. He would be out nine days without stopping, trading six-hour shifts with the captain.

Butler, like the old steamboat pilots, was in supreme command of his vessel. As I talked to him, he kept working, casually but with great confidence. I was reminded of Mark Twain's passage about the supreme command of Mississippi River pilots: "Your true pilot cares nothing about anything on earth but the river, and his pride in his occupation surpasses the pride of kings."

Being a pilot was hard sometimes, Butler said. "You lose track of what landlubbers do. You think 'river river river' night and day for weeks on end." After a whole month on the river, Butler gets only fifteen days off. It is very hard on his family, he said, but he's been doing nothing else for nineteen years.

The Gilda Sherden *maneuvering its barges.*

Springfield Plantation

Slave quarters at Springfield.

Plantation

Near the Natchez Trace, the wilderness road that ran from Natchez, Mississippi, to Nashville, Tennessee, I came across a restored cotton plantation called Springfield. Surrounded by magnolia trees, the plantation's mansion was where President Andrew Jackson had been married.

The old place had been fixed up by a descendant of the French explorer La Salle. Arthur La Salle said he grew up in New Orleans. The mansion had been used as a hay barn before he went to work. The first night he slept in the house he heard footsteps. Then he saw his door handle turn, but when he rose to see what it was, there was no one there. He told me that sometimes he still hears loud crashes that shake the whole house.

Before the Civil War, wealthy plantation owners lived in mansions along the Mississippi River from Natchez down to New Orleans. Huge profits from sugarcane, tobacco, and cotton depended on slave labor. After the Civil War, slavery was abolished and the economic system of the south changed forever. Many of the plantations went to ruin

I walked a hundred yards down the road and found some of the slave quarters intact. Occupied as recently as the 1960s by the granddaughter of a slave, the building seemed freshly lived in. I stepped inside to find three empty rooms and two cats. I got a chill thinking how hard life must have been for the slaves who once lived in these cramped quarters.

Big ships take command of the river.

New Orleans.

Ocean Ships

As I approached the end of the river, the weather turned nasty. Hurricane Georges was now only 385 miles southeast of New Orleans and heading northwest—straight for the Mississippi Delta. In Baton Rouge, the capital of Louisiana, I found workers on monstrous freighters and tankers from all over the world making fast with anchors and ropes to shore. These boats were bigger than anything I'd seen so far. From here down to the Gulf, the Corps of Engineers maintains a forty-five-foot deep-water channel for ocean-going ships. This is a highly industrial part of the river. In fact, one of my great discoveries about the Mississippi was the amount of industry along its banks. The area from Baton Rouge to the Gulf is perhaps the most industrial of all. Refineries and chemical plants line the riverbank for miles.

New Orleans, Louisiana

An eerie light filtered through the clouds from the oncoming hurricane as I headed quickly for New Orleans.

One hundred miles southeast of the city, off the coast of the Mississippi Delta, Hurricane Georges, with winds of 110 miles an hour, was kicking up seas that now ran thirty-one feet high. With 75 percent of the city below sea level, New Orleans is extremely susceptible to hurricane damage. Twenty-foot

41

Jazz bands, such as the John Robichaux Orchestra (1896), helped develop a uniquely American music.

Hurricane coming: people line up for last-minute supplies.

flood walls and levees have been built to protect the low-lying city from the rising Mississippi River on one side and from Lake Ponchartrain on the other. But if this hurricane hit dead on, as was expected, the city would be flooded from both sides. Fear of the hurricane was rising, and I grew tense as I approached New Orleans.

Perhaps it is fitting that this big river finally rolls past such an exotic city, with its rich gumbo of African, French, and Caribbean cultures. And what a city it is! One of the busiest ports of entry in the United States, New Orleans is a metropolis of food, music, and myth.

In 1722, New Orleans became the capital of the French colony. Forty years later it was transferred to Spain. With the Louisiana Purchase in 1803 the city was finally taken over by the United States. But French, or Creole, influence remains today.

New Orleans soon became a major marketplace for slaves and cotton. African Americans have been an important influence in the city ever since. It was here, in the late nineteenth century, that black musicians developed a uniqely American music called jazz.

The day I drove into New Orleans, more than a million people were evacuating the city. The highway heading north was jammed to a standstill with five miles of cars. People were trying to flee the hurricane, but the highway south into the city was a ghost road. I settled into the lovely but deserted French Quarter, the historic downtown district with old French buildings and wrought-iron balconies.

The oncoming hurricane emptied the New Orleans streets.

Boarded up: the city prepares for the storm.

By five o'clock the bridges and highways leading into the city were sealed off. No one could leave or enter. As I walked through the strange silence of the French Quarter, past Jackson Square, where the Louisiana Purchase had been signed, I noticed a few tardy shop owners boarding their windows and sandbagging their doors. Long lines had formed outside grocery shops. Everyone was trying to stock up on a few day's food in case the worst happened.

By eight o'clock that night the city was a ghost town. The temperature was a muggy ninety degrees. I secured my canoe to the ceiling of the hotel garage so it wouldn't float away in the coming flood. Then I took a walk down to the Mississippi. Amazingly, the mighty river seemed less threatening than the oncoming hurricane. Workers on supply boats huddling along the shore were madly battening down, securing lines, and getting ready to ride out the gale-force winds. The sky darkened, and the river started forming whitecaps.

Late at night, I finally fell asleep to the sound of the howling wind. I fully expected to wake to a city in flood. First thing in the morning I planned to canoe on Bourbon Street, home of Dixieland Jazz.

But miracle it was, I woke to good news! At the very last minute, the eye of the hurricane had veered to the east, bypassing New Orleans by a few miles. Tropical force winds up to seventy-five miles per hour and flooding rains were drenching the city, but the storm's fury had loosed itself on the Mississippi coast near Biloxi.

New Orleans had been spared once again.

The River's End

GRADUALLY THE SUN CAME OUT, and timid tourists emerged from their hotels. Roads and bridges were opened to traffic, and the city sloughed off its battle-zone panic. Instead of paddling on Bourbon Street, I paddled on the river, which was especially busy as the tows and supply boats went back to work. I now felt confident canoeing the Big River along the shore of New Orleans.

Outside the levee protection system, I met a writer who lives in a house on stilts. The Mississippi had risen so much during the hurricane that it lapped at the eight-foot stilts that held his tiny house above the river. Macon Fry told me he loved living this close to the Mississippi. Yesterday's hurricane had deposited a lot of driftwood, which Macon now prepared for a bonfire. He told me that sometimes when the water is high he finds "loads of alligators" on the sand beneath his home.

In the afternoon I drove down the shipping channel a hundred miles southeast of New Orleans to Venice, the last town on the Delta before the open water of the Gulf. Closer

After the hurricane, I paddled the shore.

to the eye of the storm, Venice had seen one-hundred-mile-an-hour winds and a ten-foot rise of water. Roofs had been torn off trailers, and many trees had been blown down. Now the people of the Delta were at work putting their lives back together.

Scores of helicopters flew workmen back and forth to the big oil rigs moored offshore. Shrimp boats of all sizes were getting ready to shrimp again.

The end of the Big River, the huge tidal swamp of alluvial mud, mangroves, and cypresses festooned in Spanish moss, is one of the world's great estuaries where fresh and salt water meet. Millions of ducks live here. French-speaking Cajuns, whose ancestors came long ago from Nova Scotia, catch oysters, crawfish, and crab. They also trap muskrats, otters, and nutria, or "swamp rat." Alligators live in the salt marshes, too, lots and lots of alligators.

Now it was time to return home. One thing I'd learned from adventuring out on the Big River was that my fear had dwindled as my curiosity grew. I saw more clearly how the Mississippi is both a mythic river and a real, working river. I had felt its mystery beneath my boat. I had seen its majesty from top to bottom—from the northern pines of Minnesota to the tropical mangroves of Louisiana.

Mark Twain was right. He said the river was like a book with new stories to tell every day. I vowed to return to the Mississippi. The Father of Waters has a lot more stories to tell.

For Jean Craighead George

Text and photographs copyright © 2000 by Peter Lourie
except where noted.
All rights reserved

Published by Caroline House
Boyds Mills Press, Inc.
A Highlights Company
815 Church Street
Honesdale, Pennsylvania 18431
Printed in Hong Kong

Publisher Cataloging-in-Publication Data

Lourie, Peter.
    Mississippi River : a journey down the father of waters / by
Peter Lourie. 1st ed.
[48]p. : col. ill. ;   cm.
Summary: An exploration of one of America's great rivers, from its
headwaters in Minnesota to its mouth at the Gulf of Mexico.
ISBN 1-56397-756-7
1. Mississippi River —Pictorial works—Juvenile literature.
2. Mississippi River—Description and travel— Juvenile literature.
[1. Mississippi River.   2. Mississippi River—Description and travel.]
I. Title.
976.81 -dc21   2000   AC   CIP
98-88235

First edition, 2000
The text of this book is set in 13-point Janson Text.

10 9 8 7 6 5 4 3 2 1

The author wishes to thank the following individuals for their help in the creation of this book: Connie Smith Cox, lead naturalist, Itasca State Park, Minnesota Department of Natural Resources; James T. Lovelace, Chief, Hydrologic and Hydraulics Branch (retired) U. S. Army Corp of Engineers, St. Louis District; John Shepard, Assistant Professor and Assistant Director of Hamline University's Center for Global Environmental Education in St. Paul, Minnesota; Claude Strauser, Chief, Hydrologic and Hydraulics Branch, U. S. Army Corp of Engineers, St. Louis District; Henry Sweets, Mark Twain Home Foundation.

Additional photographs courtesy of:
Jim Bailie: pp. 19, 21 (right); Monte Draper: p. 11 (top), 12; Bob Greenlee: p. 15; Hogan Jazz Archive, Howard-Tilton Memorial Library, Tulane University: p. 42 (top); The Library of Congress: pp. 10 (bottom), 14, 23, 25 (left), 27, 34, 36; Mark Twain Home Foundation: p. 24; Morrison Country Historical Society: p. 13; G. H. Suydam Collection, and Lower Mississippi Valley Collections, LSU Libraries, Louisiana State University, Baton Rouge, LA: 37 (bottom); U. S. Army Corps of Engineers: pp. 20 (right), 22 (bottom), 26, 30.